and the
Monstrous
Moon Mites

John Lomas-Bullivant

WALKER
BOOKS

Chief Engineer Samson

Moon Mite

Captain Mack

Marty Meddler

The Mayor

Tracy Trickster

Grabby Crabby

Yolanda Yummy

Peter Patent

Daisy Digger

First published 2010 by Walker Books Ltd
87 Vauxhall Walk, London SE11 5HJ

2 4 6 8 10 9 7 5 3 1

Text copyright © 2010 John Lomas-Bullivant
Illustrations copyright © 2010 Walker Books Ltd

Design and illustrations by Dynamo Ltd

The right of John Lomas-Bullivant to be identified as author
of this work has been asserted by him in accordance with the
Copyright, Designs and Patents Act 1988

This book has been typeset in Kronica Regular

Printed and bound in China

British Library Cataloguing in Publication Data:
a catalogue record for this book is available from the British Library

ISBN 978-1-4063-2366-5

www.walker.co.uk

www.captainmack.co.uk

Meanwhile, Chief Engineer Samson stays behind...

Samson calling Captain Mack. Come in, Captain Mack.

I hear you loud and clear, Samson. What's the latest news?

It's not only the astronauts who are waiting for you!

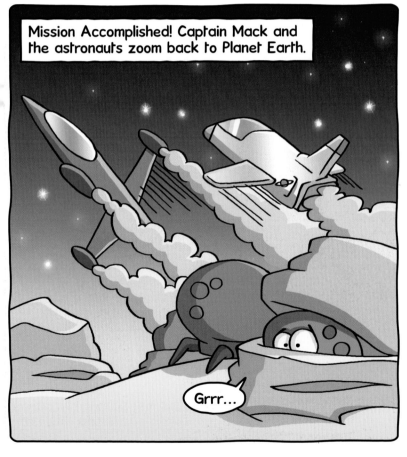

Captain Mack sets off on another exciting mission...

But will he really be able to control the weather?

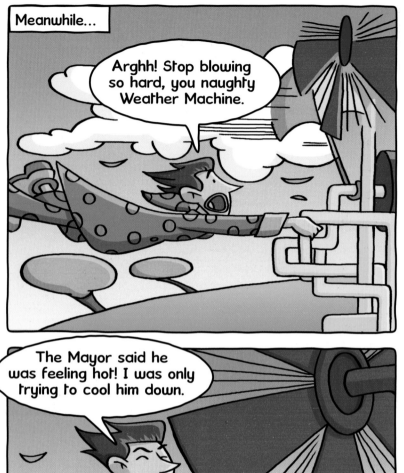

But…

I can't believe I can't find anyone to help. I'm such an excellent helper. Where has everyone gone?

Ah-ha! Peter Patent's Weather Machine is still here. I know! I'll take it back to him.

Moments later...

Hello, Grabby Crabby. Have you borrowed my Weather Machine?

I'm far too cold to borrow anything. What's going on? Sunshine City is f-f-f-freezing.

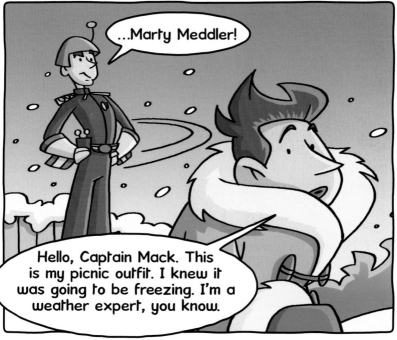

My Sky Captain powers tell me that Marty Meddler isn't telling the truth!

I'm going to get to the bottom of this.

Outside Peter Patent's house...

So, here's The Weather Machine. It's set to Super Cold! It's frozen solid!

Hurray! It's sunny again.

Sunshine City is back to normal!

TO BE CONTINUED...